The ANCESTOR TREE

by T. OBINKARAM ECHEWA

illustrated by CHRISTY HALE

LODESTAR BOOKS DUTTON • NEW YORK

to children everywhere,
who sometimes may feel an urge
to better a tradition they have received

—T.O.E.

for Scott
—C.H.

AUTHOR'S NOTE

The Ancestor Tree is an original "contemporary folktale." I call it
a contemporary folktale because I believe that Africans of this
generation cannot be content with merely retelling the folktales
bequeathed to us by earlier generations, but must, in our turn,
add to the existing tradition and produce newer stories for our
children and grandchildren.

The inspiration for the story came from a statement made years
ago by a character in my novel, *The Crippled Dancer.* "Everyone,
in time, becomes an ancestor," the character said, "even thieves
and murderers." This statement so startled me that I carried it
around for years. *The Ancestor Tree* works out its implications.

The artwork was done in linocut combined with watercolor and
color pencil on Rives Cream.

Library of Congress Cataloging-in-Publication Data
Echewa, T. Obinkaram.
   The ancestor tree / by T. Obinkaram Echewa; illustrated by Christy Hale—1st ed.
    p. cm.
   Summary: Sad after the death of their special friend, the very old man who had
told them stories and jokes, the village children decide to go against custom and
plant a tree for him in the Forest of the Ancestors.
   ISBN 0-525-67467-5
   [1. Nigeria—Fiction. 2. Friendship—Fiction.] I. Hale, Christy, ill. II. Title
PZ7.E1965An 1994
[E]—dc20   93-7205
                                                   CIP
                                                   AC

Published in the United States by Lodestar Books,
an affiliate of Dutton Children's Books,
a division of Penguin Books USA Inc.,
375 Hudson Street, New York, New York 10014

Published simultaneously in Canada
by McClelland & Stewart, Toronto

Editor: Rosemary Brosnan Designer: Christy Hale
Printed in Hong Kong First Edition 10 9 8 7 6 5 4 3 2 1

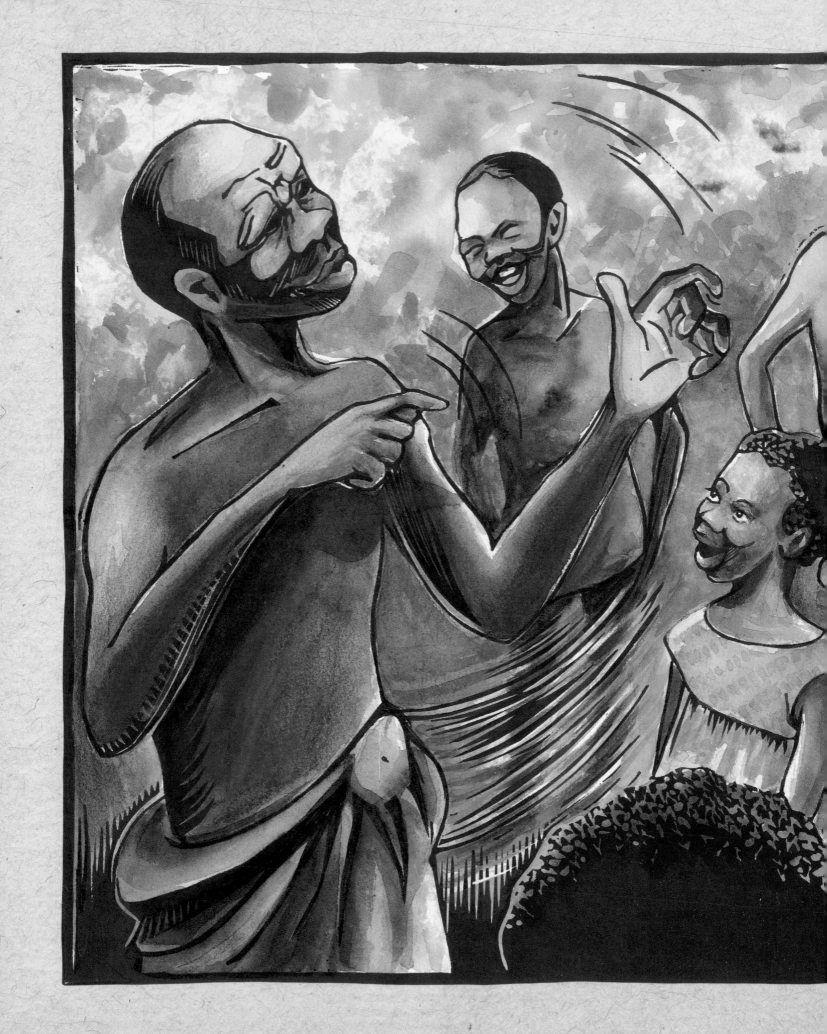

na-nna was the oldest man in the village of Amapu. He was so old that no one knew how old he really was or remembered a time when he was young. He was old, yes, but full of life. Often sick, yes, and sometimes unable to walk because of his painful joints, but always full of jokes and laughter. Often tired, yes, but never too tired to tell a story. And when he had a story to tell, the children stood in a group in front of him, joking and laughing.

His full nickname was Nna-nna Anya M'ele, which meant Grandfather the Onlooker, a funny nickname since he was blind.

"Who is blind?" Nna-nna would ask, pretending to be angry. "All I do now is *see*. I see, whether my eyes are open or closed, whether it is night or day, whether I have a lamp or not!"

It was true! Nna-nna could "see" quite well. He did not use a cane to get around, and yet he rarely stumbled. When the children came to visit him in the shed in front of the house where he spent his days, he usually greeted them by name before they even said a word. If the children had an argument while they were playing and came running to Nna-nna to settle it, he had no difficulty deciding who had started the trouble, who had first called the other person a bad name, or who had struck the first blow.

Ask or tell Nna-nna anything, and his eyes would stretch or crinkle and his tongue would waggle back and forth across his lips. And then he would give a clever answer. Sometimes, the children, especially Adindu, Aham-Efula, and Ugochi, tried to sneak up on Nna-nna, but none of them could fool him.

Every morning, even before the sun came up, Nna-nna was already sitting in his shed, scrubbing his teeth with a chewing stick, spitting into the dust, and swatting flies with his towel. The children ran up to the shed to say "good morning" to him as soon as they emerged from their houses. Adindu was usually the first one up, followed by Ugochi, Aham-Efula, and the others.

"Nna-nna, good morning!" Adindu would say.

"Nna-nna, *ifutala ulo!*" Ugochi would say.

"Nna-nna, *ibola chi!*" Aham-Efula would call out.

One by one, the children would kneel down in front of
Nna-nna and open their hands in the shape of a bowl to receive
his blessing.

"May you live a long life," Nna-nna would say, blowing into
Adindu's hands.

"Ugochi, may your bowl overflow with blessings all day long!
Aham-Efula, may Luck smile on you all day today."

"Thank you," each child would say in turn. "The same to you,
Nna-nna."

A short time later, one of the children would say, "Nna-nna, tell us a story! Tell us how we used to act when we were little babies!"

"Let me see," Nna-nna would say, and then he would begin calling the children's names one by one.

"Adindu, on the day you were born, you were so eager to come into the world that your mother nearly had you at the farm."

The children would burst out laughing, even though they had heard all this before. "What about me? What about me?" they would all say at the same time.

"Ugochi, you have always been a troublemaker. Even while you were in your mother's womb, you used to kick so much it looked like there was a war going on in there. Everyone thought your mother was carrying twins and that two of you were fighting.

"Aham-Efula, everyone knows of your loud voice! When you were born, all of the villagers heard your first cry—it was so loud!"

"Nna-nna, what about me?" the other children would shout excitedly.

"Nna-nna, how did I crawl when I was a baby?"

"Nna-nna, what was the first word I ever said?"

"Nna-nna, was I bald or did I have a lot of hair when I was born?"

Nna-nna would answer all the children's questions one by one by one.

At night, when it was time to go to bed, the children would beg Nna-nna for another story. "Just one more!" they would say as their mothers came to drag them away.

"All right, just one more," Nna-nna would agree. But as soon as he finished that story, another child would say, "Just one more, Nna-nna."

"No more, no more," Nna-nna would finally reply, laughing. "It will soon be morning, and you can all come back then."

For Adindu, Ezinna, Chidinma, Aham-Efula, Okoro, Ugochi, Adanma, Amadi, Okezia, and all the other children in the village, Nna-nna was like the sky—always there. He was there early in the morning when they woke up, during the middle of the day while they were playing, and late at night when they got ready to go to bed. It seemed that he would always be there.

Then, one day, Nna-nna became very sick. He no longer came out to the shed to sit beside his log fire, but instead lay grunting and groaning inside his house. Adults began telling the children to stay away from his door and not to bother him with their noise and anxious questions. From the secret whispers of the adults, the children began to suspect that Nna-nna was about to die.

On a day when no adults were around, the children, led by Adindu, went inside Nna-nna's house.

"Ah," Nna-nna said, as soon as he "saw" the children. He turned on his cot and began to call their names one by one. "I am very glad you have all come to visit me," he said.

"We are sorry that you are sick," Adindu said on behalf of the other children. "Is there anything we can do for you?"

"No, thank you, Adindu," Nna-nna replied, trying to shake his head. "My time has finally come, and I am going to die. But that is not why I am sad."

Several of the children began to cry.

"Why are you sad?" Adindu asked.

"Mmmmh," Nna-nna grunted. "You are children. I do not think you would understand."

"Tell us about it, Nna-nna," Adindu said, trying not to cry. "Tell us about it. We will understand!"

Nna-nna bit down on his lip as he said, "I am afraid that after I am dead no one will remember me."

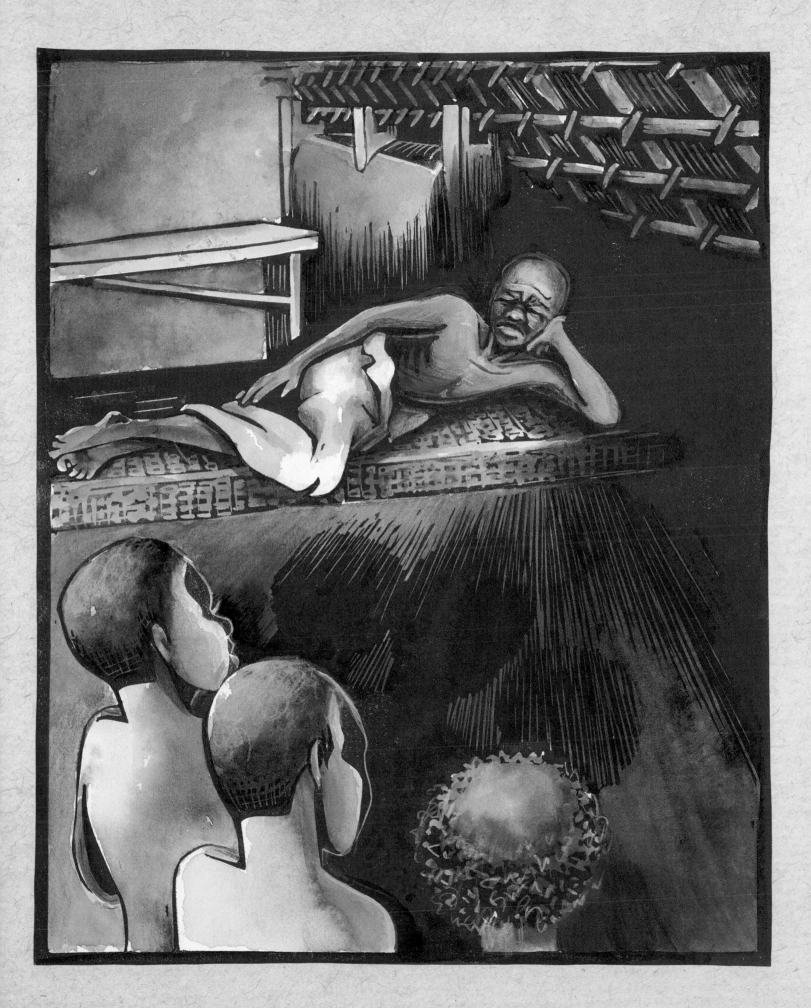

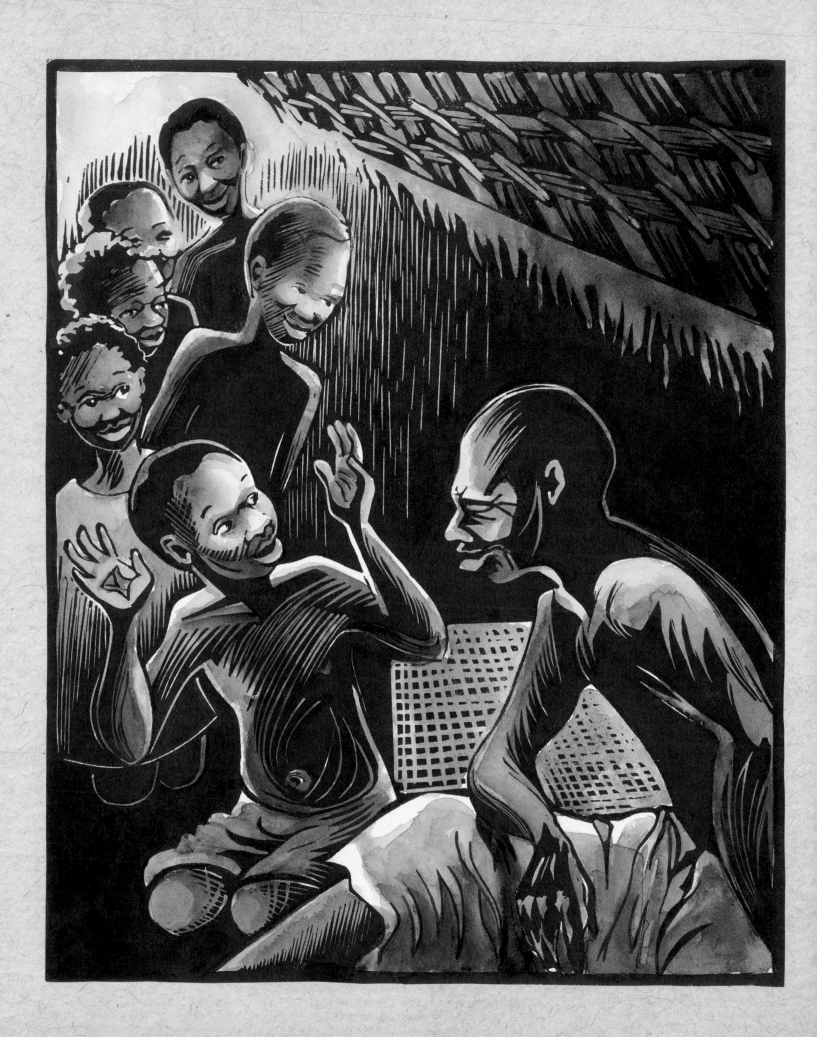

"No! No! Never! No!" the children said together. "We will always remember you. We will never, never, never forget you! We will always remember the stories you told us. Your songs and your jokes. All the games and riddles."

"Is that so?" Nna-nna asked. His voice had the hint of a laugh in it, and his eyes were crinkled, the way they always were when he was about to tell a joke.

"Yes! Yes! Yes!" the children replied.

"In that case, then," Nna-nna said, trying to laugh, "each of you must tell me a story, a joke, or a riddle—your favorite—by which you will remember me after I am dead. Adindu," Nna-nna said, "why don't you take the first turn?"

After Adindu had told his story, the other children took turns telling jokes, stories, and riddles. When they were finished, Nna-nna said, "Thank you very much, children. Thank you. As long as you remember and repeat all those stories, jokes, and riddles, I guess I will never be forgotten."

But then after a while, Nna-nna's face became sad again. The children noticed tear drops at the corners of his eyes.

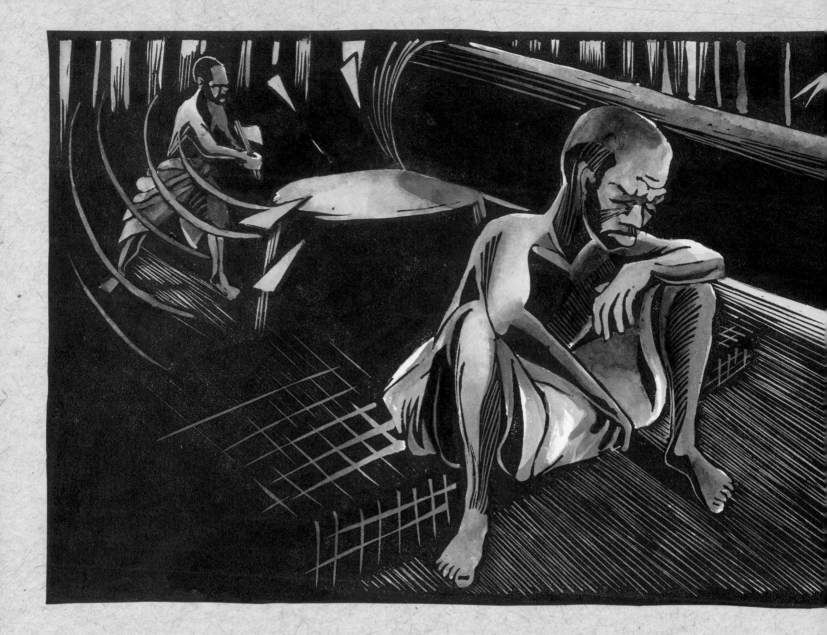

"Nna-nna, why are you still crying?" Adindu asked,
wiping the tears from his own eyes.

"The reason I am sad is that after I die my Navel Tree will
be cut down from the Forest of the Living, and no Ancestor
Tree will be planted for me in the Forest of the Ancestors!"

"O-o-oh," the children gasped. All of them knew about
the old custom of planting Navel Trees and Ancestor Trees.
Their village had two sacred forests, the Forest of the
Living and the Forest of the Ancestors. Whenever a child

was born in the village, a piece of that child's navel cord was planted together with a young tree in the Forest of the Living. And whenever anyone from the village died, that person's Navel Tree was cut down, and a new tree, called an Ancestor Tree, was planted for the person in the Forest of the Ancestors. However, there was one condition for planting an Ancestor Tree: The person who died had to have living children.

Nna-nna had no living children.

"Do not cry, Nna-nna," Adindu said. "I am sure there is something we can do."

"There is nothing you can do," Nna-nna replied. "Custom is custom. I cannot say that it should be changed because of me."

"We will always remember you, Nna-nna, no matter what," Adindu said.

"Yes," Ugochi agreed. "We will never, never forget you!"

Aham-Efula spoke next. He said, "If the adults do not plant an Ancestor Tree for you, we will sneak into the Forest of the Ancestors and plant one. By the time anyone finds out, your tree will already be there!"

"Yes," Adindu agreed. "All of us will sneak into the forest together, and we will not be afraid. And if we cannot plant an Ancestor Tree for you right away, we will plant one for you when we grow up."

"I appreciate your kind thoughts, children," Nna-nna said. "I may not have a tree in the Forest of the Ancestors, but I am glad to know that I will be alive in your memories. All of you together will be my Ancestor Tree."

About a week later, Nna-nna died. That same night, his old Navel Tree was cut down.

For days afterward, all the children in the village were sad. When they woke up in the morning, Nna-nna was no longer in the shed waiting to say "good morning" to each of them and blow a blessing into their hands. At night, when they finished their moonlight games and were about to go to bed, Nna-nna was no longer there to tell them "just one more story," or to call out funny good-nights to them as their mothers dragged them to bed.

Every day, the children gathered in Nna-nna's shed to talk about him and tell his stories and riddles to one another. Sometimes, they held contests to see who remembered more of Nna-nna's jokes. At other times, they took turns pretending to be Nna-nna, saying and doing the things he used to say and do.

Inside their homes, when they were with their fathers and mothers or uncles and aunts, the children kept asking, "How come Nna-nna can't have a tree in the Forest of the Ancestors?"

"It is an ancient custom," Adindu's father said when Adindu asked him.

"How come there is such a custom?" Adindu asked.

"That's just the way things are. Custom is custom is custom," Adindu's father replied.

"How do customs begin?" Adindu persisted.

"I do not know. Most customs are so old they started even before I was born."

"Do customs ever change?" Adindu asked.

"Enough questions!" Adindu's father replied angrily. "Go and find something to do."

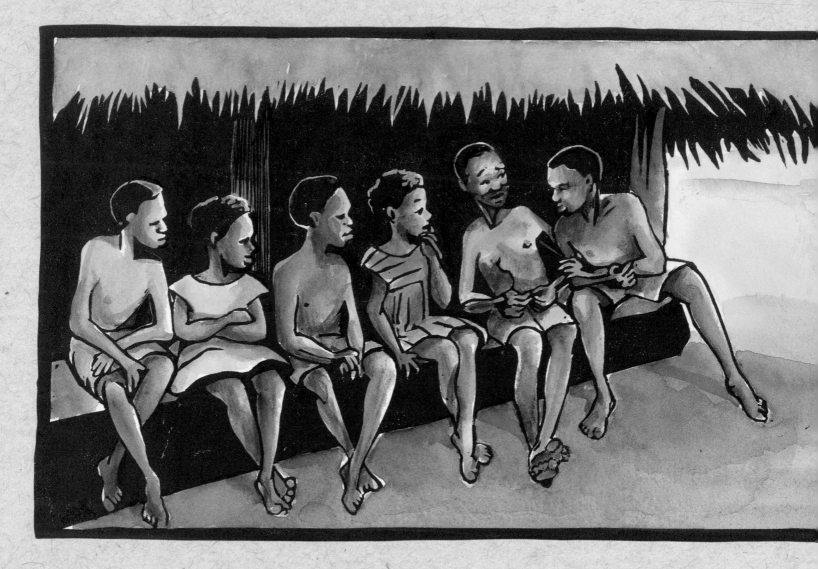

One day, while the adults were holding a Village Council meeting nearby and the children were playing in Nna-nna's shed, Ugochi said, "Nna-nna has been dead now for many weeks, and still no Ancestor Tree has been planted for him."

"That is true," Aham-Efula said, "but what can we do? We are only children."

"But we promised Nna-nna that we would do something," Ugochi reminded everyone.

"That is true," Adindu said, holding his head in his hands and thinking deeply.

"But what can we do?" Aham-Efula asked again.

"Let us be bold," Adindu said suddenly, his eyes burning with determination. "The adults are having their meeting. Why don't we go over there now and ask them to plant an Ancestor Tree for Nna-nna?"

"No-oh," many of the children said, shrinking back in fear. "Children are not allowed at the adults' meeting."

"I know," Adindu said, "but are we going to break our promise to Nna-nna?" When Adindu asked this question, many of the children became silent and sad. After a while, they agreed to go with Adindu and began walking slowly toward the Village Council.

"What is the matter?" asked Ozurumba, the oldest man at the Council. "Why are you children walking around with such sad faces? We realize that your friend, Nna-nna, died recently, but everyone dies sooner or later, and Nna-nna lived a very long life."

Adindu raised his hand, and Ozurumba nodded to him to speak. "We are sad," Adindu said, "not only because of Nna-nna's death but because no Ancestor Tree has been planted for him in the Forest of the Ancestors."

"That is true," Ozurumba said. "We cannot plant an Ancestor Tree for Nna-nna because he is not an ancestor. He has no living children."

"But all the children want Nna-nna to be *our* ancestor,"
Adindu said. "All of us feel like his children and grandchildren."

"Is that so?" Ozurumba asked, his eyes widening with
surprise.

"Yes," Adindu replied.

"I see," Ozurumba said. He and the other adults in the
Council were surprised by the children's boldness and, for a
long time, continued to shake their heads in disbelief. After
talking for a while among themselves, they told the children
to come back in a week to hear the decision of the Council.

The children were very excited as they walked away.

A week later, the children returned.

"Ezi, amuru!" Ozurumba said, as the children held their breaths in anticipation. "Teach and learn. Usually, adults teach and children learn, but in this case, we have the opposite. Children are teaching and adults are learning. You children have taught us that customs have a beginning, customs can change, and sometimes, customs come to an end. We have decided to end one custom and begin another. We will plant a tree for Nna-nna in the Forest of the Ancestors. It is true that he has no living children, but it is also obvious that he has left something of himself in all of you, which, after all, is what it means to be an ancestor."

Ozurumba continued: "We have also decided that, from this day onward, we will change the way we select which ancestors to honor. Beginning today, only people who have lived honorable lives, people whose spirits are noble, will have trees planted for them in the Forest of the Ancestors. *Ezi, amuru* indeed!"

The children were very happy. They jumped up and down, hugged one another, and exchanged pumping handshakes. But above all, they were proud of what they had accomplished. Nna-nna would not be forgotten.